For Ethan, Quinn and Arwyn. **LW.**

Many thanks and love to Shay for the love and support. **DS.**

First published by Albert Street Books, an imprint of Allen & Unwin, in 2021

Copyright © Text, Lili Wilkinson 2021
Copyright © Illustrations, Dustin Spence 2021

All rights reserved. No part of this book may be reproduced or transmitted in any form or by any means, electronic or mechanical, including photocopying, recording or by any information storage and retrieval system, without prior permission in writing from the publisher. The Australian *Copyright Act 1968* (the Act) allows a maximum of one chapter or ten per cent of this book, whichever is the greater, to be photocopied by any educational institution for its educational purposes provided that the educational institution (or body that administers it) has given a remuneration notice to the Copyright Agency (Australia) under the Act.

Allen & Unwin
83 Alexander Street
Crows Nest NSW 2065
Australia
Phone: (61 2) 8425 0100
Email: info@allenandunwin.com
Web: www.allenandunwin.com

 A catalogue record for this book is available from the National Library of Australia

ISBN 978 1 76087 739 2

For teaching resources, explore www.allenandunwin.com/resources/for-teachers

Cover and text design by Kristy Lund-White
Set in 15 pt Yearnboy11 by Kristy Lund-White

Printed and bound in April 2021 by McPhersons Printing Group, Australia

10 9 8 7 6 5 4 3 2 1

 The paper in this book is FSC® certified. FSC® promotes environmentally responsible, socially beneficial and economically viable management of the world's forests.

HOW TO MAKE A PET MONSTER
FLUMMOX

LILI WILKINSON

Illustrations by DUSTIN SPENCE

CHAPTER

Have you ever wanted a **pet monster?** If you are like me, the answer is **NO**, because **monsters don't exist.**

If you are like Willow, the answer is **YES DEFINITELY.**

I am Artie.

This is Willow.

This is the **BIG**, **SPOOKY** house that we live in together, with my mum and Willow's dad.

And this is Hodgepodge, my pet monster. (Apparently monsters **DO** exist? I am as surprised as you are.)

Willow and I found an ancient spell book called **THE BIGGE BOKE OF FETCHING MONSTERS**, which shows you how to make **REAL MONSTERS**. Hodgepodge was supposed to be a **hobgoblin**, but we couldn't find the ingredients listed in the spell book, so we used things from around the house and got Hodgepodge instead. I'm glad, because Hodgepodge is my **best friend**.

Now Willow wants to make a monster of her own, and I'm a bit scared.

When we made Hodgepodge, I didn't believe in monsters.

I didn't think anything would happen,

because I know about Science, and I know that you can't just *make* a monster, and also that monsters aren't real.

Except we did make a monster, and now he is **SLEEP-FARTING** on the end of my bed.

Now that I know monsters **ARE** real, I'm worried about making a new one. **'What if it is dangerous?'**

'I hope it is,' says Willow. 'Let's get to it. I want this one.'

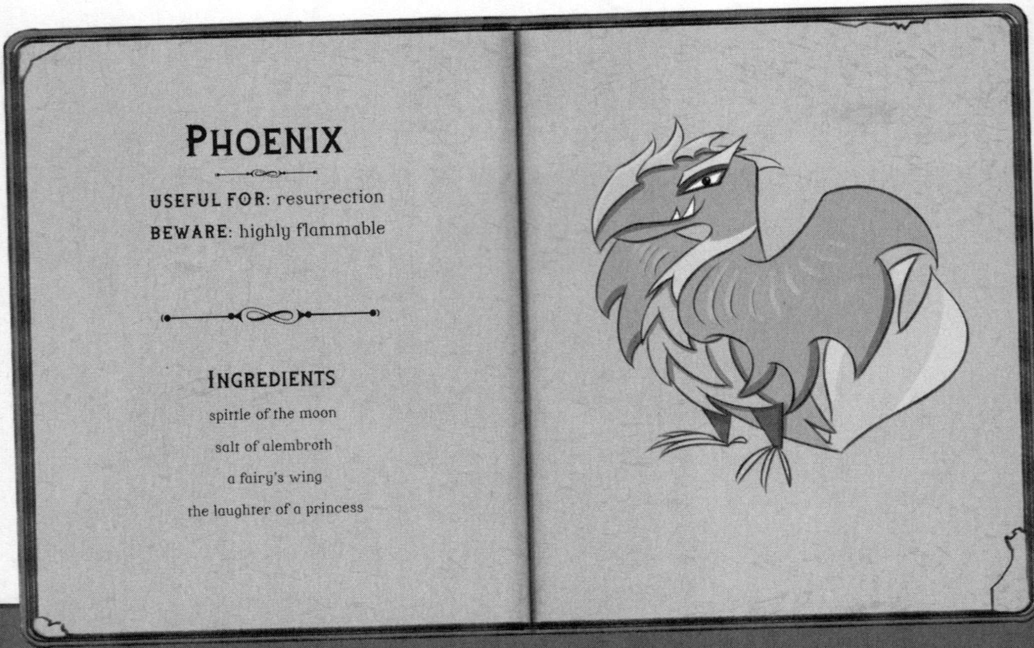

Phoenix

USEFUL FOR: resurrection
BEWARE: highly flammable

Ingredients

spittle of the moon

salt of alembroth

a fairy's wing

the laughter of a princess

'First we need **spittle of the moon**,' says Willow.

'That's impossible,' I tell her. 'The moon doesn't have salivary glands.'

'Sure,' says Willow, shrugging. 'But **YOU** are **MOON-FACED**. So you can just spit in the kettle.'

I open my mouth to argue, but Willow has her determined face on, so instead I lean over and

SPIT into the kettle.

'Right,' says Willow, examining **THE BIGGE BOKE OF FETCHING MONSTERS**. 'Next we need **salt of alembroth**.'

'What's alembroth?' I ask.

'Who cares?' Willow replies. 'Regular salt will do.'

I hope I never have to do a real **SCIENCE** experiment with Willow. **IT WOULD GO VERY <u>BADLY</u>.**

'I'll get the salt,' Willow says. 'You can get the **fairy's wing.**'

'Ah,' I say. 'Well, I can't do that. **Because there is no such thing as fairies.**'

Willow opens her mouth to reply, but she's interrupted by my mum calling us from downstairs.

'Artie! Willow! There's someone here I want you to meet.'

'I'm *so* happy to meet you all,' says Arabella-Rose.

Willow and I exchange a look.

'Arabella's parents are out of town, and her uncle got held up coming to collect her, so she is going to spend the day with you two. I know you'll make her feel welcome,' Mum says, giving Willow and me a firm look as she leaves the room.

Arabella-Rose perches on the sofa like a QUEEN. 'Go on, then,' she says.

'Err,' I reply.

'We're supposed to be getting to know

each other. Don't you want to ask me some questions?' she says.

Willow makes a **snorting noise**. 'Here's a question. What time are you going home?'

This is a **VERY RUDE** thing to ask, and Arabella-Rose narrows her eyes at Willow. But she quickly smiles and says, 'My Uncle Cranky is picking me up at five-thirty. He's not really cranky. He's lovely. I just call him that to be funny.' Arabella-Rose laughs at her own joke and continues. 'He's not really my uncle, either. He's my great-uncle once removed. Do you know what "once removed" means? I can explain all about ancestry if you'd like.'

Suddenly, five-thirty feels like a long time from now.

WILLOW LOOKS FURIOUS. I would bet my subscription to Junior Scientist

Magazine she is annoyed that we can't make her monster while Arabella-Rose is here. I am secretly relieved. Arabella-Rose might be **SNOOTY**, but she doesn't look nearly as **SCARY** as a **real live monster**.

Arabella-Rose doesn't seem to notice the tension. 'Here are some interesting things about me,' she says. 'I am twelve years old. My favourite colour is gold. I don't like spiders or cottage cheese. I'm going to be an actress and a singer. I brought my scrapbook of all the different performances I've done, and all my favourite shows. Would you like to see it? Would you like to hear me sing now?'

She doesn't wait for an answer, just launches into a song I've never heard before but seems to be about castles and clouds.

I think Arabella-Rose is actually a pretty good singer, but **Willow looks like she's going to PUKE**. Which is weird, because Willow loves music. Maybe they could do a duet?

Arabella-Rose pauses to take a deep breath, and Willow jumps in. 'That was so pretty, Arabella. I'm sure your grandparents *love* that one. Do you know any songs by **DEATH RATTLE SPIDER?** I can play "Snort Face" on the guitar.'

Arabella-Rose glares at Willow. 'I'm sure "Snort Face" is great for a *beginner*, but my mum says music should lift your soul, so I only sing *actually good* music.'

'Oh really?' says Willow. 'Perhaps you should have lifted that last note a little, it sounded flat to me.'

Arabella-Rose blushes **BRIGHT RED**. But only for a second.

'How tragic that you don't have a good ear for pitch, Willow.

That must make it really hard to play your guitar. You are so brave for trying your best anyway.'

'I'm going to my room...to do some... homework,' Willow says, through gritted teeth.

Arabella-Rose narrows her eyes. 'It's the school holidays.'

'I like to get started early.'

Just when I think I might have to come up with a plan to distract them, I see a flash of green fur from the corner of my eye. **OH NO.**

'What kind of homework is it?' asks Arabella-Rose.

'Um. Maths.'

'I'm **really** good at maths. I'll come and help you.'

The flash of green is **HODGEPODGE**, who has come to see our visitor. I shake my head at him. **It's better if people don't know about Hodgepodge.** A man called **WESLEY CRANKSHAW** found out about him, and tried to steal him and put him in a cage. We had to rescue him.*

Arabella-Rose gets up to follow Willow, and Hodgepodge ducks behind a cushion on the couch.

'No!' Willow says. 'I don't want your help.'

Arabella-Rose's chin wobbles. 'You're supposed to play with me,' she says. 'That's why I'm here.

* Read book 1 for this adventure!

I'm going to be here all day, **so you'd better start being nicer.'**

'Can't you go to an actual friend's house?' Willow asks. 'Or don't you have any?'

Willow is being super mean. We just moved here, so it's not like we have any friends either.

'I HAVE HEAPS OF FRIENDS,' says Arabella-Rose firmly. 'They're just… all… busy.'

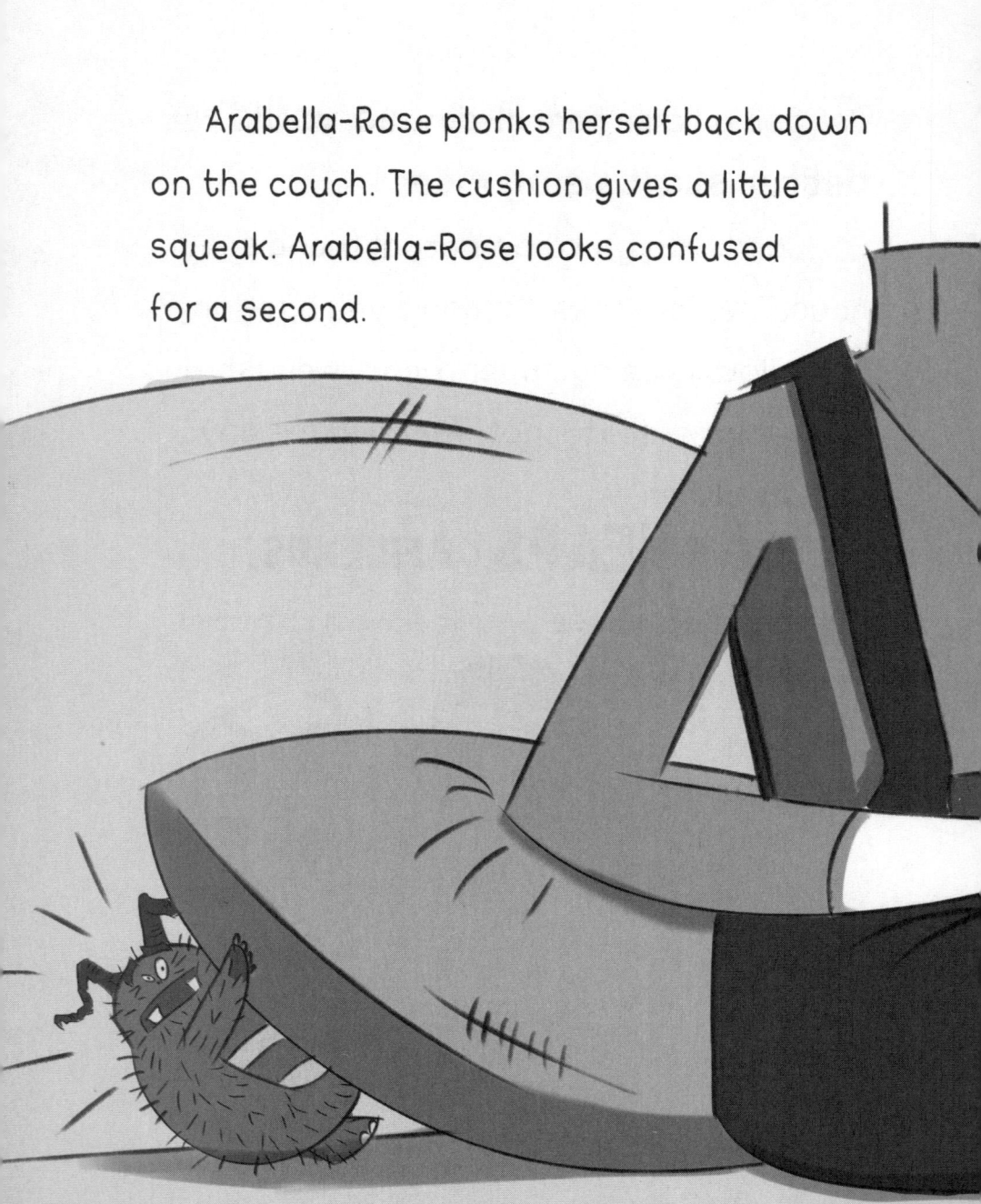

Arabella-Rose plonks herself back down on the couch. The cushion gives a little squeak. Arabella-Rose looks confused for a second.

'Your mum said you were supposed to make me feel welcome.'

'Indira isn't my mum.'

'You're not being nice.' Arabella-Rose glares at Willow.

'Why don't you play with Artie?' Willow suggests with a fake smile.

Arabella-Rose's cheeks go pink and she stands up. 'I'm going to tell your parents that you're being mean.'

Hodgepodge appears from behind the cushion, looking a bit squashed. Arabella-Rose turns around, but he whisks himself behind a fat teapot on the shelf.

'What was that?' Arabella-Rose asks.

'What was what?' Willow responds.

'That furry thing. It looked...kind of like a...furry monster?'

'It was Hodgepodge.' I am very bad at lying.

Willow shakes her head at me.

'WHO IS HODGEPODGE?' asks Arabella-Rose.

CHAPTER 2

'A TEDDY BEAR,' Willow says. 'Hodgepodge is Artie's teddy bear.'

'Let me see,' demands Arabella-Rose.

But Willow grabs Arabella-Rose's arm and pulls her out of the room. 'Let's play **Hide and Seek**,' she calls over her shoulder. 'Artie, you're it!'

'Stay hidden,' I tell Hodgepodge sternly. **'Don't let Arabella-Rose see you.'**

Hodgepodge nods seriously, then does a **BLUE CHEESE FART**, and scurries away.

I count to fifty, then start to look for Willow and Arabella-Rose.

I look in the kitchen, but I only find Willow's dad, David Cole.

'Are you kids having a good time?' he asks. 'I'm making deep-fried porridge.'

David Cole loves cooking weird things. Some of his favourite dishes are

'We're playing hide and seek,' I reply, so I don't have to answer the question.

I look in the dining room, but there's only Mum looking at paint samples.

'Do you think the library walls should be painted in Disco Salmon, or Funky Banana?' she asks.

I look in the bathroom, but there's only our old cat, Murphy, asleep in the sink.

I stop at the top of the basement stairs. I don't like the basement. It's too **DARK** and **SCARY**.

'She didn't go that way,' says Willow from behind me, making me jump.

'You're supposed to be hiding!' I say.

'I am,' she says, walking towards me. She whispers, 'I'm hiding from Arabella-Rose.'

'That doesn't sound very fair,' I say.

'What isn't *fair*,' says Willow, 'is that we have to babysit **Miss Princess** all day, when we should be making my monster. I've got the salt. Have you figured out the fairy's wing yet?'

I open my mouth to remind her that fairies aren't real, but Arabella-Rose appears.

'You took too long to find me,' she says. **'I got BORED. This house is BORING.'**

'What do you usually do at friends' houses?' I ask.

'Oh, the usual,' says Arabella-Rose. 'We sing songs from musicals and make up dance routines and eat cupcakes. That's the kind of thing I do all the time with all my friends.'

Willow narrows her eyes.

'Did somebody say cupcakes?' David

Cole asks, poking his head into the hallway. 'I just made a batch to test out my curry caramel crush icing. Do you kids want to decorate them?'

Arabella-Rose makes a face. **'Curry icing?'** she says. **'That sounds gross.'**

'You can just use regular icing if you want,' David Cole says.

'I *love* curry icing,' says Willow fiercely.

David Cole looks surprised.

In the kitchen, Arabella-Rose slips her charm bracelet off her wrist and puts it on the bench. 'Uncle Cranky gave me this,' she says. 'I can't get it dirty.'

'Can I have a look?' Willow asks.

Arabella-Rose nods and Willow picks up the bracelet. 'It's really beautiful.'

Now I am surprised. Willow doesn't seem like a charm bracelet kind of person. I lean over her shoulder to see the bracelet.

It's gold, with lots of tiny, delicate charms.

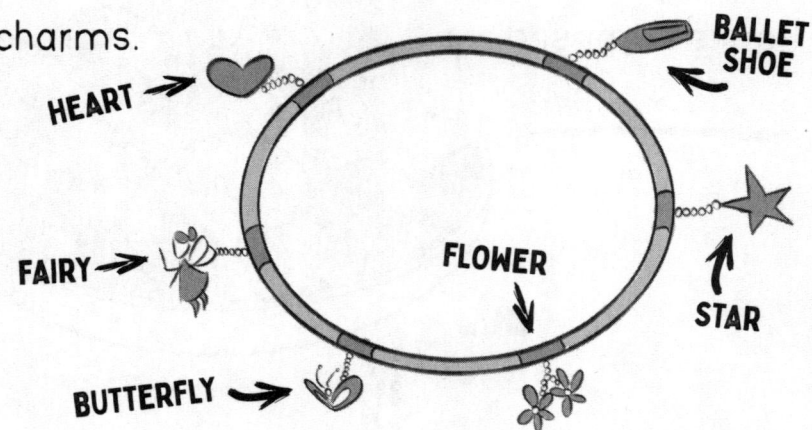

OH.

There is a fairy charm on the bracelet.

And Willow needs a fairy's wing for the monster recipe.

But that would be *stealing*, and **stealing is wrong**.

I frown at Willow, a frown that says, *Do not steal Arabella-Rose's precious bracelet.*

Willow smiles at me. It's a **SCARY** smile.

I open the pantry to get some sprinkles, and notice a **VERY STRONG FARTY SMELL**.

Hodgepodge is there on the top shelf, happily munching on a cabbage.

'You're meant to be hiding!' I whisper, putting a large bag of flour in front of him.

We decorate our cupcakes, and for a little while I forget that I have a pet monster hiding in the pantry, and that Willow is desperate to make her own monster and is hatching some kind of **DEVIOUS PLAN**.

Willow nudges me. 'Do you remember the last thing on the ingredient list?' she whispers.

'The laughter of a princess?'

Willow nods, then jerks her head at Arabella-Rose, who is frowning at her cupcake. She *is* the princessiest person I've ever met. **BUT HOW DO WE CAPTURE HER LAUGH?**

Willow holds up an almost-empty jar of David Cole's parsnip and lime marmalade.

'Make her laugh,' she hisses.

Arabella-Rose doesn't seem to be in much of a laughing mood. She is doing a lot of complaining.

'I can't make my icing roses look good without a proper piping bag. Don't you have any **REAL** gold leaf?' she says. 'I can't believe these are the only sprinkles you have. When I go to my friends' houses, they have a *hundred* kinds of sprinkles.'

Willow narrows her eyes. 'What are your friends' names?'

'Err,' Arabella-Rose looks panicked. 'Elle! And Glinda. Matilda. And Eponine.'

Willow opens her mouth, and I know she's going to tell Arabella-Rose that she thinks her friends are made-up, and that *definitely* won't make Arabella-Rose laugh.

'DOES ANYONE KNOW ANY JOKES?' I say loudly.

There's a jokes page in my **Junior Scientist Magazine**, so I try a few of them out on Willow and Arabella-Rose.

Apparently I'm the **ONLY ONE** with a sense of humour around here, because **neither Willow nor Arabella-Rose laugh at ANY of my jokes.**

Then Willow drops her spoon and when she bends over to pick it up, Hodgepodge does a loud, cupcake-scented fart from behind the flour.

Arabella-Rose's eyes go wide with shock. Her mouth opens, and

AHAHAHAHAH!

ARABELLA-ROSE IS **LAUGHING**.

Arabella-Rose is laughing *at Willow*.

Willow doesn't like being laughed at.

Her face goes all scrunched-up and angry, but I nudge her in the ribs. 'The jar!' I whisper.

Arabella-Rose is still laughing. 'You... did... a... **FART!**' she giggles.

Quick as a flash, Willow grabs a half-eaten jar of marmalade from the kitchen bench, whisks it under Arabella-Rose's chin, then slams the lid on.

Arabella-Rose stops giggling. 'What did you just do?' she asks.

'Nothing.'

'You just did something weird with a jar. **IS THIS SOME KIND OF PRANK?**'

'It's none of your business,' says Willow.

Arabella-Rose looks at Willow, then at me, then back at Willow. Then she bursts into tears and runs out of the room.

'Shouldn't we see if she's okay?' I ask.

'Later,' says Willow. 'Let's go make my monster.'

CHAPTER 3

'We still don't have the fairy's wing,' I say as we climb the stairs to the attic.

'Sure we do,' Willow says, and holds up the fairy charm from Arabella-Rose's bracelet. **'WILLOW,** I say sternly. **'THAT'S STEALING!'**

Willow shrugs. 'She left it lying around. I bet she has a hundred charm bracelets at home. This is just one charm. She won't even notice it's gone.'

I'm starting to feel queasy.

Willow drops the ingredients into David Cole's black electric kettle.

'I'm so excited to meet my monster!' Willow says. 'I wonder what it will be like.'

'Hopefully not too dangerous,' I mutter.

'I'm going to call it **FANG**,' Willow says. 'Or **ROCK**. Or **AXE**.'

She opens up **THE BIGGE BOKE OF FETCHING MONSTERS** and begins to chant.

'Fetch up a creature as **wild** as can be, fetch up a **monster** and bind it to me. Fetch up and heed ye **obediently**, fetch me my bidding... **And ye will be free!**'

A wisp of steam emerges from the kettle, slowly growing into a thick steamy cloud.

Then there is a BANG, and a very strong smell of BUBBLEGUM.

Hodgepodge squeaks in fear and burrows under my arm.

When the steam clears, **there is a new monster in the room.**

The monster has silky-looking fur
and delicate moth-like antennae. It has

enormous violet eyes with long lashes. **It's really quite beautiful**, but it also looks a bit… **SILLY?**

Willow frowns. I guess she was imagining something a bit more **FIERY** and **DANGEROUS-LOOKING**.

Hodgepodge steps forward to sniff the new monster carefully.

The creature flinches away from him. Hodgepodge waves a paw at the monster and the room smells like roses. The monster looks at Hodgepodge and then around the room. It makes a nervous clucking noise.

'It looks a bit like a chicken,' I observe.

'It does *not*,' says Willow.

It totally does.

The monster opens its beak and SQUAWKS.

Like a chicken.

Hodgepodge does a squeaky fart in response and the monster waves its antennae at him.

'Hello,' Willow says gently. 'I'm your new owner.'

'I'm not sure *owner* is the right word,' I say. 'I don't *own* Hodgepodge. This is his home and he's my best friend.'

Willow gives me a look and takes a step towards the monster. The monster looks unsure.

'You have to give it a task,' I tell Willow. 'Remember?'

Willow nods and opens her mouth.

'ARTIE MULLINS AND WILLOW COLE, GET DOWN HERE THIS INSTANT!'

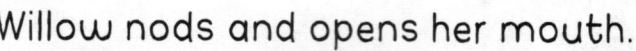

It's my mum, and she sounds really, really angry.

Willow sighs. 'Hodgepodge, stay here with the new, um, monster,' she says. 'We'll be right back.'

CHAPTER

Mum and David Cole are really, really **ANGRY**.

Arabella-Rose is sitting on the sofa in front of the TV. She has icing on her cheek and her face is all blotchy from crying.

'I can't believe you were both **SO RUDE** to Arabella-Rose,' Mum says.

Willow has her arms folded. She doesn't say anything.

'The fairy charm from my bracelet is missing,' sobs Arabella-Rose. 'My Uncle Cranky gave it to me!'

I feel really, really terrible.

It's not Arabella-Rose's fault that she came here on the same day that Willow wanted to make a monster.

And it's not her fault that her charm bracelet just *happened* to have a fairy charm on it.

And it's *really* not her fault that the

fairy charm has turned into a sort of chickenish fluffy monster.

'It will be around here somewhere,' Mum says soothingly to Arabella-Rose. Then she turns to us. 'Artie and Willow are going to help you find it. **Aren't you?**' Mum glares.

'Yes, Mum,' I say.

I hate it when Mum is angry at me.

Arabella-Rose says she's too upset to look with Willow and me, so she's going to stay in the lounge. She takes a bite of cupcake, and turns on the TV.

Willow and I go to the kitchen to look for the fairy charm, **which is SILLY,** because we know we're not going to find it.

'I told you we shouldn't have used the fairy charm,' I say, lifting the lid off a teapot. **'Stealing is wrong.'**

Suddenly, a siren wails.

'They're onto us!' I yell.

'WE'LL GO TO PRISON!'

Willow rolls her eyes. 'First of all, that's a fire engine siren. Second of all, it's on the TV,' she says.

I breathe a huge sigh of relief, but Willow is scowling.

'I never get to watch TV in the middle of the day,' she grumbles. **'Today sucks.'**

I hear a gentle **fART**, and turn to see Hodgepodge, leading the new monster into the kitchen by the paw.

'At least you got to make your monster!' I say.

Willow doesn't say anything.

The monster looks around the kitchen, and then lets out a **SQUAWK**.

Willow awkwardly pats the new monster.

'Hello, there,' she says. 'You're very... soft.'

The monster waves its antennae and giggles.

'Huh,' I say. 'That sounds a bit like Arabella-Rose, don't you think?' If Arabella-Rose's laugh was more... **chickenish**.

Willow rolls her eyes at me. 'No, it doesn't.'

Willow takes a deep breath and smiles at her monster. **'We're going to have so much fun together,'** she says, looking hopeful.

The creature waves its antennae at Willow.

Hodgepodge farts loudly, the flowery fart that means he's happy. The new monster cocks its head to one side, then opens its beak again.

A sort of farty noise emerges.

'Oh!' says Willow.

She whistles at the monster.

It whistles back.

Willow claps her hands, three times.

The monster opens its beak and a **CLACK-CLACK-CLACK** sound comes out.

'It's a mimic,' Willow says proudly. 'It can repeat sound. That's its special power!' Then her eyes light up. **'I have an idea!'**

She scoops up the new monster, who lets out a startled cluck, and hurries up the stairs to her bedroom.

'Shouldn't we be looking for the fairy charm?' I ask.

Willow makes an exasperated noise. **'COME ON!'**

Hodgepodge and I follow.

Willow takes her electric guitar out of its case and plugs it into the amp.

'Me and my monster are gonna *rock*,' she says.

She plays a loud, screechy chord.

BROWWWW

The new monster lets out a terrified **SQUAWK**, and scuttles under Willow's bed. Hodgepodge puts his paws over his ears.

'I don't think monsters like the electric guitar,' I tell Willow.

Neither do Arties. But I don't say that out loud, because Willow is looking really disappointed.

We coax the monster out again, and it stands there staring at us.

'It's waiting for a task,' I say.

'I can't think of anything,' says Willow. She's starting to look sad.

'How about a name?'

Willow looks at her monster.

'**SHREDDER?**' she suggests.

The new monster is **definitely not** a Shredder.

'**BLAZE? SPIKE? RIFF?**'

None of them are right.

'I'm sure you'll figure it out,' I say.

'Of course I will!' Willow is trying to be positive, but I can tell that things aren't going the way she imagined they would.

We hear the sound of footsteps approaching, and David Cole opens Willow's bedroom door. Willow throws a blanket over the monster. 'Aren't you two supposed to be looking for Arabella-Rose's missing charm?'

A chickenish giggle drifts out from underneath the blanket.

David Cole frowns. 'There's nothing funny about this, Willow.'

He looks like he's about to say something else, but the doorbell rings.

'That'll be my exotic fruit delivery,' he says. **'You two had better find that charm.'**

Willow doesn't look for the charm. Instead she tries to make friends with the new monster, but it isn't going very well. Arabella-Rose has stopped watching TV and is interrupting us instead, and... well, Willow and her monster don't seem to have much in common.

First of all she tries to teach it to talk. 'Okay,' she says. 'Say **"LET'S ROCK!"**'
The monster makes confused clucking sounds in response.

'I think it can only do sounds,' I tell Willow. 'Not words.'

'Well, that doesn't make sense,' she replies.

'We made a monster out of salt and spit and a fairy charm and a giggle,' I remind her. **'*None* of it makes sense.'**

'HAVE YOU FOUND MY FAIRY CHARM YET?' asks Arabella-Rose, sticking her head into the room, holding another cupcake.

'No,' says Willow, whisking the new monster behind her amp. She glares at Arabella-Rose.

Arabella-Rose makes a rude face at her and stalks off.

Willow tries playing the new monster some of her favourite rock music, turned down really low. But the new monster just looks miserable and does more sad clucking.

Arabella-Rose appears again, holding her scrapbook. **'Even looking at pictures from my favourite musicals isn't cheering me up,'** she says dramatically, before dragging her feet down the hallway. 'Definitely don't come and look with me.'

Willow looks a bit like a dormant volcano that is on its way to being not-dormant.

We sneak out to the backyard, and Willow tries to play soccer with the new monster, the way we do with Hodgepodge. But the new monster is **SCARED** of the ball. It runs away, squawking and flapping, and disturbs Murphy who is sleeping in a flowerpot.

SMASH.

YOWLLLLLL

THE WILLOW-VOLCANO RUMBLES.

The back door opens and there is a dramatic sigh. 'This never would have happened if I'd gone to one of my real friends' houses,' Arabella-Rose says. 'They are all so clever and talented. And they know how to find things properly.'

The Willow-volcano explodes.

'SHUT UP!' she yells.

'You don't even have any friends — you made them up!'

Arabella-Rose stares at her for a moment. Then she turns around and marches inside.

I glance over at Willow, but she's still boiling over. She glares at the new monster. I think… she might be going to cry? **'WILLOW COLE,'** shouts Willow's dad from inside. **'KITCHEN. NOW.'**

We go inside to find Arabella-Rose tearfully telling David Cole everything.

'I-I don't know why she hates me so much,' she blubbers. 'All I've done is tried to be h-her friend. I even tried to help her with her terrible inferior music... but all she does is say mean things.'

Willow glares at Arabella-Rose. **'I can't believe you *dobbed*.'**

Arabella-Rose bursts into fresh floods of tears. **'See?'** she says to David Cole.

David Cole pats Arabella-Rose on the shoulder. 'There, there,' he says. 'Why don't you go and wait in the living room, and I'll have a word with Willow.'

Arabella-Rose heads out of the room, but when David Cole isn't looking, she glances back at Willow and **sticks her tongue out.**

David Cole turns to Willow, his arms folded. **'I'm very disappointed in you, Willow,'** he says. 'I want you to go in there and **APOLOGISE** to Arabella-Rose.'

Willow shakes her head.

'WILLOW. YOU WILL GO IN THERE AND APOLOGISE NOW.'

Willow glares at him, at me, at the world. Then she stomps towards the living room.

'I wish Arabella-Rose would just go away,' she mutters under her breath.

Something fluffy whisks past my ankles.

'Was that Murphy?' David Cole asks as we follow Willow into the lounge room.

I don't think it was Murphy.

Arabella-Rose isn't in the lounge room.

David Cole frowns. 'I guess she needed a minute to herself,' he says. 'Wait here until she gets back.'

He wanders back to the kitchen.

I look at Willow, whose eyes are **WIDE**. 'Do you think...' I say.

Willow nods. 'I wished that Arabella-Rose would go away,' she says, her eyes wide. 'And the new monster thought that was its task.'

CHAPTER 5

Arabella-Rose has **VANISHED**, and so has the new monster.

'I should have known that new monster wouldn't get what I meant,' Willow says fiercely. 'It doesn't understand me like Hodgepodge understands you.'

'Willow,' I say carefully. 'Are you a little bit disappointed with the new monster?'

Willow glares at me, but then her shoulders slump. 'It's…It seems nice, but it's not exactly what I imagined.'

Hodgepodge farts, and I smell **CABBAGE**. If I had known I was going to have a pet monster, I never would have imagined one like Hodgepodge. But I still love him, just the way he is.

'Maybe we could swap?' Willow suggests. 'You can have the new one, and I'll have Hodgepodge.'

Hodgepodge gives Willow a **CROSS LOOK**.

In the PARLOUR.

We even go down to the

SCARY BASEMENT.

But no Arabella-Rose.

'You don't think that the new monster made her *really* **disappear**, do you?' I ask. **'LIKE...FOREVER?'**

'Definitely not,' says Willow, but she doesn't sound completely sure. 'Maybe we should look in the East Wing.'

Mum and David Cole haven't started fixing up the East Wing yet. Mum says we have to get an engineer in to make sure it's 'structurally sound' before we spend time in there.

WE ARE ABSOLUTELY *NOT ALLOWED* IN THE EAST WING.

I am suddenly very nervous. 'Maybe we should tell our parents we can't find her?'

'Yeah, right,' says Willow, and goes charging off down the hallway to the East Wing.

'Wait!' I say. 'We need a torch. Mum has turned off the electricity in that part of the house.'

I scurry back to my room and get a torch.

This is a very bad idea.

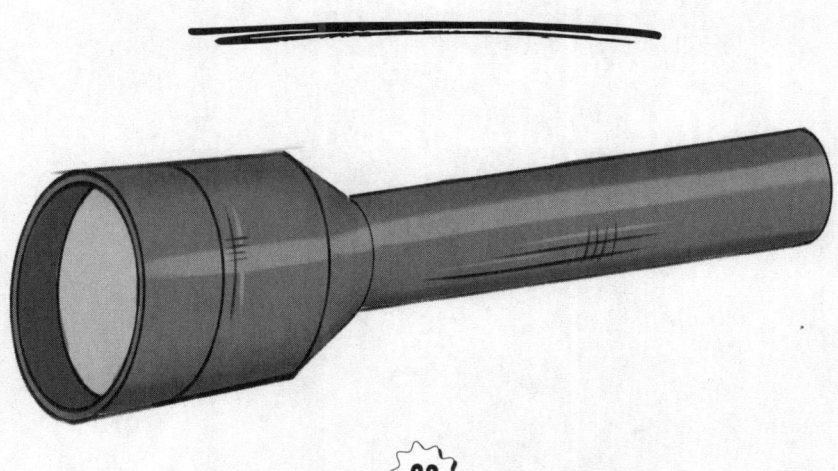

The East Wing is EVEN SPOOKIER than the rest of the house.

Everything is dusty and covered in spiderwebs. There are pieces of old furniture left over from whoever used to live here. There's a rocking chair, a wardrobe that I'm just **SURE** is full of creepy bugs, and paintings that I feel are watching as we make our way down the passage.

Willow frowns. **'Can you hear that?'**

I nod slowly. It sounds like music.
CREEPY MUSIC.
Like a ghost is playing a piano.
CREEPILY.

'Maybe we should go back,' I say.

Willow ignores me and marches down a dusty hallway to a closed door.

The music gets louder as we approach, but as soon as Willow opens the door, it stops.

We hear footsteps, and then the very distinct sound of a

IT'S ARABELLA-ROSE!

We burst into the room.

'There's no one here,' says Willow. **'Only this dusty old piano.'**

I look around carefully. 'Willow,' I say. 'We just heard the piano playing, right?'

'Right.'

'And there is only one door into this room, right?'

'Right.'

'And we heard Arabella-Rose scream, right?'

'Right.'

'So where *is* she?'

Willow's face lights up. 'Do you think a ghost was playing the piano?' she says.

'That would be *so cool.*'

I do not believe in ghosts.

However, just a few days ago I didn't believe in **monsters**.

But then I look down at the ground and notice footprints on the dusty floor. They are **ARABELLA-ROSE-SIZED.** And there are fingerprints in the dust on the piano, too.

Hodgepodge climbs up and presses one of the piano keys.

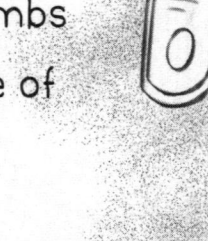
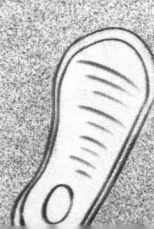

PLINK

Then another

PLONK

Then another

PLUNK

Then another—

But the last one doesn't make a noise. Hodgepodge looks confused, and presses down on the key again.

He looks up at me, then back down at the piano.

'Maybe you're not hitting it hard enough,' Willow says, and leans forward to press her own finger against the key.

This time, the piano does make a sound. But it's not a **PLONK** sound like before. This time it's a grinding, crunching noise.

The whole piano swings out from the wall, revealing an **ACTUAL HIDDEN PASSAGE** with stone steps leading down.

Willow turns to stare at me. 'This is the **greatest thing** that has ever happened.'

I **DO NOT** AGREE. This looks like the most dangerous thing that has ever happened.

'We should wait for Mum's engineer,' I say. **'WHAT IF THE CEILING FALLS DOWN ON US!'**

Willow jumps up and down a few times, and nothing even creaks. 'See?' she says. **'Solid as a rock.'**

She walks towards the opening of the passageway. 'I bet it was Arabella-Rose playing the piano,' says Willow. 'And she triggered the secret passage.'

'Well,' I say, putting on my best grownup voice, 'I think we should find her. It's not her fault we—'

Willow cuts me off with a glare. 'Of course we should find her,' she says. 'Arabella-Rose is the most annoying person I've ever met, but that doesn't mean I want to have disappeared her forever!'

For the first time, Willow starts to look a bit worried.

But she steps into the spooky passage.

I pick up Hodgepodge, take a deep breath and follow Willow.

'Are we even still in the house?' Willow asks. 'I feel like we've been walking for ages.'

I hope the torch batteries don't run out.

Eventually, the passageway stops, and we find ourselves standing at the top of what looks like a long tunnel slide.

It is smooth, **AND SLIPPERY, AND DARK.**

I don't know what I'm going to find at the bottom of the slide, but I know it's going to be

TERRIFYING.

Maybe it will be:

- a pool filled with crocodiles
- a cave full of giant spiders
- a torture chamber
- an evil wizard's laboratory
- a crypt full of ghosts

I look at Willow. Even she appears a bit scared.

But then we hear something.

A noise coming from the bottom of the slide.

A noise that sounds a bit like a kid **crying**.

'I think it's Arabella-Rose,' I say.

'Come on,' says Willow, and sits down with her bottom on the edge of the slide.

She takes a deep breath, and pushes off, disappearing into the darkness.

'WILLOW?' I yell after her.

I look down into the blackness.

'THIS IS A BAD IDEA,' I say, stepping

away from the edge of the slide. **'I'm not doing it.'**

But Hodgepodge farts an encouraging flowery fart and points down the slide.

I sigh.

'Okay, Hodgepodge. We'll do it together.'

I sit down on the edge of the slide, Hodgepodge on my lap.

I CLOSE MY EYES. I TAKE A DEEP BREATH. And we S

CHAPTER

Me and Hodgepodge shoot out of the slide, landing on an old soft cushion, in a **VERY STRANGE ROOM**.

There is no pool of crocodiles, or ancient crypt, or evil wizard's laboratory.

The room has six sides, and on each side there is a door painted a different colour. The red door we just came through swings shut behind us.

The room is crowded with comfy-looking chairs and small tables and footstools. The ceiling is painted to look like the sky at night, and I don't need my **Junior Scientist Magazine Special Night Sky Lift-Out** to know that all the constellations are in the right places.

In the middle of the stars, golden letters spell out the words

> # CRUMBLE SNOT

WHICH IS <u>WEIRD</u>.

Stretching over our heads is a set of monkey bars, and a series of small ropes and ladders. The ropes and ladders look too small for people to use, even kids.

Willow is standing in the middle of the room, looking around with her mouth open.

And Arabella-Rose is sitting in an armchair, **holding the new monster in her arms and GLARING AT US.**

'I **KNEW** there was something **WEIRD** about you two,' Arabella-Rose says. **'Your house has a dungeon!** And your pet is a monster chicken.'

The monster in Arabella-Rose's arms **CLUCKS NERVOUSLY**. Arabella-Rose hums a little tune to it, and it hums back. It sounds sort of **shimmery** and **beautiful**, the notes blending and harmonising with Arabella-Rose's voice.

Willow is watching them. I've seen that look on her face before, when she realised that she couldn't get her parents back together. She looks a bit like her heart is breaking.

'We've never been to this part of the house,' I say quickly. 'What is this room?'

'I don't know,' Arabella-Rose replies. **'FLUMMOX** brought me here. It's pretty cool, isn't it?'

'Flummox?' Willow says.

'Flummox,' Arabella-Rose says proudly, pointing at the new monster. 'I didn't know her name, so I started calling her Flummox, because it just *felt* right, and she really seemed to like it. I think she's beautiful. You are so lucky.'

FLUMMOX HUMS HAPPILY.

Hodgepodge steps out from behind my legs and farts cheerfully, Arabella-Rose's eyes light up. 'I *knew* that wasn't your teddy bear!' she says. 'What's his name?'

'Hodgepodge,' I tell her, and Hodgepodge waves.

'Where did you get him?' Arabella-Rose asks.

'Well,' I begin, at the same time as Willow says, **'None of your business.'**

Willow scowls at me. 'Don't tell her anything, Artie.' She walks towards Arabella-Rose. 'And that's **MY** monster you're holding.'

The monster squawks as Willow reaches out to snatch it.

'Hey!' says Arabella-Rose. 'Be gentle with Flummox. She's very shy.'

'How **DARE** you give her a name,' Willow says. 'That's supposed to be my job.'

'Oh, I'm *sorry*,' says Arabella-Rose hotly. 'What's her name, then?'

Willow opens her mouth, then shuts it again. She can't think of a name.

I put on my Scientist voice and say, 'Flummox *does* suit the new monster. "Flummox" means to confuse someone, like you're not quite sure what's going on, and...' I gesture at Flummox, who is quite beautiful but also quite chickenish. 'She looks a bit confusing. And a bit...confused.'

Willow scowls at me again and quickly turns away.

Hodgepodge is exploring the room. There's a big table in the middle, and shelves around each of the doorways. Most of the shelves are empty, but some of them are cluttered with dusty jars or crumbling old books. There are lots of pictures on the walls, of different kinds of terrifying-looking monsters.

'I wonder if the person who owned **THE BIGGE BOKE OF FETCHING MONSTERS** kept their monsters in here,' I say thoughtfully.

I examine the doors more closely, and

notice that none of them have locks or handles or anything. I push on one, but it won't budge.

I'm starting to get a bit worried. If none of the doors open, then how are we going to get out?

'This never would have happened if you hadn't run off,' Willow says to Arabella-Rose.

'I didn't run off. Flummox came and got me. And she has been **MUCH** nicer company than you!'

'Excuse me,' I say.

Arabella-Rose and Willow look at me.

'We are stuck in a weird underground chamber and my careful examinations have not found a way out,' I tell them. 'That is quite enough to deal with. **PLEASE STOP FIGHTING.**'

They look back at each other but don't say anything.

I walk over to the paintings on the wall. There's something weird about one of them.

All the other ones are portraits of monsters.

But the painting next to the yellow door is of the very room we are standing in. **That seems WEIRD.**

I narrow my eyes and look carefully at the painting.

HARPY

OOZLUM BIRD →

SELKIE →

SPHINX

BANSHEE

'There's something about this picture...
'The words on the ceiling!' I say suddenly. 'They're different!'

Willow comes over to look. **'NUMBER CLOTS,'** she reads. 'And our ceiling says **CRUMBLE SNOT**. Is it a mistake?'

'I think it might be a clue?' I say.

Arabella-Rose comes over to look too. 'My Uncle Cranky likes to do cryptic crosswords, and he taught me a little bit. I think that's an **anagram**, which is when you use all the same letters to make different words.'

I look up at the ceiling. The letters look like they can be taken off and moved around, but it's too high for us to reach.

'Hodgepodge,' I say, 'do you think you could climb up to the ceiling?'

Hodgepodge looks up and farts anxiously. He doesn't like heights. But before he can even try, Flummox **whisks** up the ladders and ropes, and balances on the monkey bars. She lets out a triumphant squawk, and a clapping sound.

'GREAT WORK, FLUMMOX!'

Arabella-Rose says.

Willow clears her throat. 'Yeah!' she says. 'Well done…Flummox. Now, can you rearrange the letters?'

Flummox pulls the letters off one by one with her beak, and looks down at us, waiting.

'Okay, Flummox,' I shout up at her. 'Try **NUMBER CLOTS**.' I spell it out for her.

Nothing happens. 'What about **TUMBLE CORNS**,' Arabella-Rose says. 'That's all the same letters too.'

'How about **STOLEN CRUMB**,' suggests Willow, spelling it out.

Nothing.

We shout up a couple more combinations.

MOLTEN SCRUB

CURLS ENTOMB

'What exactly do you think is going to happen?' Arabella-Rose asks.

'I don't know,' I admit. 'But the painting must be a clue.' I close my eyes and concentrate on the letters. Then I suddenly realise. 'Flummox, try **MONSTER CLUB!**'

Flummox rearranges the letters again.

I hold my breath.

There's a click, and the yellow door swings open.

We cheer, and Flummox scampers down to perch on Arabella-Rose's shoulder, looking **very proud** of herself.

Willow looks a bit sad as Flummox

preens on Arabella-Rose's shoulder, but she shakes it off.

'**Monster Club!**' she says. 'You were right, Artie. I bet **THE BIGGE BOKE OF FETCHING MONSTERS** person made this room.'

'If it was a monster club,' Arabella-Rose says, 'it must have been more than one person. Maybe there were six people, one for each door. And each of them had a different monster?'

She reaches up a hand to stroke Flummox's soft fur.

'Come on,' says Willow. 'Let's get out of here.'

We head through the yellow door and find...

Stairs. LOTS OF STAIRS.

Willow, Arabella-Rose and Flummox disappear up the stairs. Hodgepodge and I take one last look around the funny room, then start heading up the stairs too.

WE CLIMB AND CLIMB AND CLIMB.

And eventually come to a little tunnel, which leads to a ladder.

And we climb the ladder.

And at the top of the ladder there is a trapdoor.

We push it open and find ourselves in a garden.

But it's not our garden.

Our garden is overgrown and jungly, with the big fig tree and long grass.

This garden is neat and perfect, with flowerbeds and roses and little gnome statues everywhere.

Arabella-Rose gasps.

'This is *my* garden!'

CHAPTER 7

How did we end up in Arabella-Rose's garden?

Hodgepodge starts to enthusiastically munch on flowers, but Arabella-Rose gasps again.

'Oh no!' she says, pointing.

A car is pulling up in the long driveway. It's a very fancy car, all shiny and big with dark-tinted windows.

'That's Uncle Cranky's car!' she whispers. 'It must be nearly five-thirty. I'll get in trouble if he finds out I was here without an adult. We have to get back to your house!'

I try to get a look at the famous Uncle Cranky, but all I can make out is a tall figure behind the steering wheel.

The car stops, but the tall figure doesn't get out. Instead, we hear the sounds of a very screechy opera coming from inside. I can see the tall figure waving his arms around, like a conductor.

Hodgepodge does the stinky sock fart that he makes when he's anxious.

I guess he doesn't like opera.

'Is there a back gate we can use?' Willow asks.

Arabella-Rose shakes her head. 'It's locked. The only way out is down the driveway.'

And Uncle Cranky is in the driveway, listening to opera in his car.

We'll have to be really sneaky.

'Come on Hodgepodge,' I whisper, **BUT HODGEPODGE WON'T BUDGE**. He shakes his head and does more **SOCK FARTS**.

'What's wrong?' I say, holding on to his hand to pull him along. 'We have to go!'

Reluctantly, Hodgepodge follows us as we get down low and creep along the side fence, hiding behind bushes and statues. Hodgepodge lets out the occasional little squeak of fear. Flummox sticks close to him, letting out reassuring clucks.

I don't understand why Hodgepodge is so scared. Mum's renovations are at least twice as loud as the opera.

Just as we pass the car, the opera singer lets out a particularly high note, and Hodgepodge lets out a particularly stinky sock fart.

A *really* loud one.

The opera turns off, suddenly, and Uncle Cranky's car door opens. I see an expensive-looking black boot step onto the driveway. Then another.

Those boots look familiar.

Hodgepodge's eyes are wide and he is trembling with fear.

Arabella-Rose whispers something to Flummox, who whisks under the car and scuttles off to the other side of the driveway.

The boots take one step towards the bush where we're hiding.

THEN ANOTHER STEP.

Then, there is a loud farting noise from the other side of the car from where we are hiding.

'Hmm?' says Uncle Cranky.

There's something **very familiar** about his voice.

I hear the farting noise again. Hodgepodge is safe in my arms, so it must be Flummox using her mimicking skills.

The big black boots turn and walk around the back of the car to the other side.

Flummox scurries under the car, back to us.

'Run!' whispers Willow, and we all dash down the driveway.

As soon as we make it back to our own spooky house, we race up to my bedroom.

'Phew!' says Arabella-Rose, panting. **'That was close!'**

'Good thinking, with the distraction,' Willow says to Arabella-Rose and Flummox.

Flummox looks very proud of herself, and I'm a bit proud of Willow. It took all day, but she finally managed to say something nice to Arabella-Rose.

'Does this kind of thing happen to you two a lot?' Arabella-Rose asks.

'Only since we moved here,' Willow says. 'A horrible animal collector tried to steal Hodgepodge from us and put him in a cage. It was a whole thing.'

Arabella-Rose frowns. 'An animal collector?'

'Yeah,' I tell her. 'He was awful. He had this huge mansion but kept the animals in cages. The cages were pretty fancy,' I admitted, 'but it was still wrong! So we rescued Hodgepodge and set all the other animals free.'

I say it like it was no big deal, like we

go on huge animal rescue missions all the time and are generally very brave and exciting. But Arabella-Rose doesn't look impressed. She frowns thoughtfully at me instead.

There's something niggling at the back of my mind, and I can't figure out what it is. Something to do with Hodgepodge being so scared in Arabella-Rose's driveway.

Something to do with those fancy-looking black boots.

There's a loud knock at the door, and Mum calls out, 'Arabella-Rose, you have a visitor!'

Arabella-Rose's face brightens and she skips off downstairs.

We hear her say, 'Uncle Cranky!'

And we hear another voice say, 'Hello, Arabella-Rose. Have you had a good day?'

And I know that voice.

I turn to Willow, who has a horrified look on her face.

'Uncle Cranky,' she whispers. 'Do you think…?'

We run downstairs just in time to see Arabella-Rose standing up on tiptoes to give her Uncle Cranky a hug.

She looks so pleased to see him.

Willow and I are not pleased to see him.

We are not pleased at all.

Because Uncle Cranky is **Wesley Crankshaw, RARE ANIMAL COLLECTOR AND KIDNAPPER OF MONSTERS!**

Where is Hodgepodge? I try not to panic but I can't let Wesley Crankshaw get his hands on my monster again.

An anxious farting noise makes me sigh with relief. Hodgepodge peers around the corner to see Wesley Cranskhaw, then scurries away to my bedroom.

'Thank you for having me,' Arabella-Rose says sweetly to Mum. She looks over at us. 'Thanks for making me feel *so welcome*,' she says, with a glint in her eye.

Wesley Crankshaw is staring at me and Willow. He has a glint in his eye too. 'What a lovely house you have, Indira,' he says, smiling at Mum. 'It has real... **POTENTIAL**.'

My skin crawls. He knows where we live, now. We'll have to be extra careful keeping Hodgepodge and Flummox safe.
FLUMMOX!

I hear Crankshaw saying goodbye to Mum and see him turn to leave, but all I can think about is Flummox. *Where is she?*

Arabella-Rose waves goodbye, then turns and follows Wesley Crankshaw down the garden path.

And sticking out of her backpack is a tuft of silky fur.

CHAPTER 8

'Arabella-Rose has *stolen* my monster!'

Willow is angry.

Willow is **very angry**.

Willow is **SO ANGRY** that I'm worried she might explode.

I open my mouth to say something soothing.

But I can't think of anything.

Willow is right.

Arabella-Rose *did* steal Flummox.

And even though Arabella-Rose and Flummox seem to get along a lot better than Willow and Flummox do, **it's not okay to steal a monster.**

On the other hand, Willow stole Arabella-Rose's fairy charm. And that was definitely not okay. And Willow still hasn't made it right.

I don't know what to think.

'We've got to get her back,' Willow says, **'before Wesley Crankshaw puts her in a cage.'**

We need to find a way to get into Arabella-Rose's house without Wesley Crankshaw seeing us.

Luckily we know a **secret way**.

The back door is open, and we sneak in.
Arabella-Rose's house is quite posh.

The carpet is fluffy and beige, and there are beige cushions and beige vases *everywhere*. Everything seems very clean. And very beige. Our house has cat hair all over the place, and spiderwebs and muddy footprints. But there's also lots of colourful teapots and furniture and photos of me and Willow when we were little. And scraps of paper with David Cole's handwritten recipes everywhere. And all Mum's university degrees framed on the wall.

    This house doesn't look very kid-friendly. I wonder how Arabella-Rose can play without knocking over a vase or staining a beige rug.

I have to pick Hodgepodge up, to stop him from eating the flowers.

There are voices coming from another room, and Willow and I crouch down.

'I'm so sorry,' Wesley Crankshaw is saying, 'but your parents won't be back tomorrow after all. They have more business meetings in the city.'

'Oh,' says Arabella-Rose in a small voice.

We creep forward and peer around a door to see Arabella-Rose sitting at a piano. Wesley Crankshaw is watching her play. There's no sign of Flummox.

'Can I come and stay at your house?' Arabella-Rose asks.

Wesley Crankshaw hesitates. 'Err, my house is a little messy right now.'

Willow snorts quietly. **We left a bit of a MESS at Wesley Crankshaw's house when we rescued Hodgepodge.**

'But I'll stay here with you,' Crankshaw says. 'I *do* have some things to attend to during the day, so perhaps you could go to a friend's house?'

Arabella-Rose looks down at her feet. 'I don't have...There isn't really anyone.'

'I *knew* it!' Willow hisses. 'I *knew* she was lying about all her friends.'

But somehow Willow doesn't look all that glad about being right.

'What about those two children you played with today?' Wesley Crankshaw asks. 'They seemed very...nice.'

The way he says it makes a shiver run down my spine.

'I don't think they liked me very much.'

'**NONSENSE,**' says Wesley Crankshaw firmly. 'How could anyone not like a **brilliant, talented** girl like you?'

Arabella-Rose swallows. 'Are Mum and Dad going to miss my music concert tomorrow night?' she asks.

'They are going to try their very best to

make it, but they might miss it. But you *know* I'll be there. **FRONT ROW!** Cheering the loudest for my little star.' Wesley Crankshaw squeezes Arabella-Rose's hand.

Arabella-Rose makes a sad little sniff.

'And we can call them before the show, and straight after,' Crankshaw continues and Arabella-Rose sniffs again, but she looks a bit cheered up.

'Maybe I could get a sneak preview right now?' Wesley Crankshaw suggests.

Arabella-Rose smiles a small smile, then turns around on the piano stool. She takes a deep breath and starts to play the piano and sing.

Wesley Crankshaw closes his eyes and hums along.

It's weird to see him being so nice.

'Come on,' Willow whispers. 'Let's look for Flummox.'

We creep past the beige living room and up a big beige staircase.

We see a room with a sign on it that reads

Arabella-Rose

We push the door open.

Arabella-Rose's bedroom is *not* beige.

It is very sparkly. There are posters from musicals all over the walls, and trophies from dance competitions. I see her scrapbook lying on her bed, along with her backpack.

And Flummox, perched like a queen on a shiny golden pillow.

'FLUMMOX!' Willow rushes towards her. **'Are you okay?'**

Flummox does her soft clucking giggle.

'What are *you* doing here?' says a voice behind us.

Arabella-Rose is standing in the doorway. She steps into the room and closes the door behind her.

'You **STOLE** my monster!' Willow grabs Flummox off the pillow. 'We are **RESCUING** her.'

Flummox squawks indignantly.

'I didn't *steal* her,' Arabella-Rose says defensively. 'She hid in my bag. I didn't realise until I got home.'

'You don't even know that you've put her in danger. I bet you don't know that your Uncle Cranky collects rare animals. I bet you don't know that he has a secret room for magical creatures, and that he'd do *really bad things* in order to own one.'

Arabella-Rose looks a bit taken aback. Then she puts her hands on her hips. 'I *do* know that Uncle Cranky collects rare animals,' she says hotly. 'But he **LOVES** them. **He'd never do anything to hurt them.**'

Willow opens her mouth to disagree, but I cough loudly. I don't like Wesley Crankshaw either, but it can't be very nice learning that your favourite uncle puts friendly monsters in cages.

'Anyway, I haven't told him about Flummox,' Arabella-Rose says, crossing her arms.

Willow stops short. **'Y-you haven't?'**

Arabella-Rose shakes her head. 'Of course not. Flummox isn't like a turtle or a lizard. **YOU CAN'T PUT HER IN A CAGE.** I was going to bring her back to you tomorrow.'

Willow isn't quite sure how to respond to this.

'I love my uncle,' Arabella-Rose says. 'But I don't tell him *everything*. I'm not a monster.'

Hodgepodge squeaks indignantly.

'Sorry, Hodgepodge,' Arabella-Rose tells him. 'I didn't mean it like that.'

Hodgepodge lets out a vinegary fart, and Flummox **GIGGLES**.

Willow scowls, and looks like she

might cry. 'Your fairy charm made my monster into a silly giggling chicken!' she says. 'You ruined *everything*.'

Arabella-Rose stares at her. 'My fairy charm?' she says. **'You... YOU took my fairy charm?'**

And then they start yelling at each other.

I feel something boiling up inside me. Hodgepodge does an anxious sock fart. I just wish Arabella-Rose and Willow would stop fighting.

'I wish I'd never had to come to your big spooky old house!'

'Well, *I* wish you'd never come too, with your silly charm bracelet and your silly scrapbook.'

'ENOUGH!' says a loud, angry voice, and I'm surprised to realise that it's **my voice**. Arabella-Rose and Willow turn to stare at me. **'You've been fighting ALL DAY.** You're both being rude and selfish. We are here to rescue Flummox, and all you can do is shout at

each other. **And look, you're scaring Flummox!**' I gesture to Flummox, who is hiding under the golden pillow, her fluffy tail sticking up.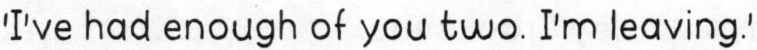
'I've had enough of you two. I'm leaving.'

And with that, Hodgepodge and I stomp out of the room, down the stairs and **SMACK BANG** into Wesley Crankshaw.

Quick as a flash, he snatches Hodgepodge, who struggles and farts loud, terrified anchovy farts.

'Give him back!' I shout.

But Wesley Crankshaw doesn't give

Hodgepodge back. He grabs a big glass vase, and shoves Hodgepodge inside.

'It's really lovely to see you again, Artie,' says Wesley Crankshaw, with a fake smile. 'Lovely of you to bring Hodgepodge to visit my niece.'

The vase shakes in his grasp, but he holds on tight.

'The last time we saw each other, you had just ruined my life's work,' Wesley Crankshaw says bitterly. 'Remember? When you destroyed my entire rare animal collection?'

'We didn't *destroy* it,' I retort. 'We set them free. You'll never be able to lock them up again, just like you'll never be able to lock up our monsters!'

Wesley Crankshaw's eyes go very bright. 'Monsters, *plural*?' he says eagerly. **'You mean there's more than one?'**

Too late, I remember that Willow told Wesley Crankshaw that **THE BIGGE BOKE OF FETCHING MONSTERS** crumbled to dust after we made Hodgepodge.

He didn't think we could make more monsters.

But I just told him we could.

There's a gasp behind us, and I turn to see Willow and Arabella-Rose staring at us. There's no sign of Flummox, thank goodness. Arabella-Rose looks from me to Wesley Crankshaw, to Hodgepodge, stuck in the vase.

'Uncle Cranky!' Arabella-Rose shouts. **'What are you *doing*?!'**

Wesley Crankshaw goes red and suddenly looks guilty. 'Bella, darling,' he says quickly. 'This is a very special creature, and I—'

'**Oh, I will,**' says Wesley Crankshaw with a smile. 'But as I said, he's very special. And I want something special in return. Say the magic monster-fetching book?'

Willow shoots me a look. '**NO WAY,**' she says fiercely.

'I'll get it,' says Arabella-Rose.

Everyone stares at her.

'I'll get the book for you, Uncle Cranky,' she says. 'But I am **so upset** at seeing poor Hodgepodge like that. Do you *promise* you'll give him back?' Arabella-Rose's eyes look shiny.

Wesley Crankshaw opens his mouth

but Willow scoffs at Arabella-Rose. 'You don't even know where it is.'

Arabella-Rose smiles coldly at Willow. 'You left me alone in your weird house all day. Did you think I was just watching TV?' She turns back to Crankshaw. **'I know where it is, Uncle Cranky.'**

Willow stares at her, her fists clenching. **'DON'T DO IT, ARABELLA-ROSE,'** I say. 'That book is **powerful**. You don't know what he might do with it.'

Wesley Crankshaw snorts. 'And you think it's better off in the hands of a couple of *kids*?'

Arabella-Rose looks from me to Willow.

There is a glint in her eyes. 'I'll just pop over and get it now, shall I, Uncle Cranky?'

And then she skips from the room.

Wesley Crankshaw narrows his eyes at us. 'I think it's best if you two wait in the bathroom,' he says. 'So you can't get up to any mischief.'

He herds us into a fancy bathroom and shuts the door. There is a clicking sound as he locks it.

CLICK!

WE'RE IN REALLY, REALLY BIG TROUBLE.

CHAPTER 9

To pass the time, I try to name all the moons of Jupiter. The big ones are easy – Io, Europa, Ganymede and Callisto.

Willow is very quiet.

I don't know what time it is. Will our parents be worried?

What if Wesley Crankshaw calls them and tells them we're staying for dinner?

They'll believe him, because he's a grownup.

I close my eyes.

HERMIPPE SINOPE ERINOME KALE

'What are you muttering about?' Willow asks.

I explain about the moons. 'There are seventy-nine altogether. Some of them don't even have names yet.'

'What? Why haven't they named them? Are the scientists too busy? I could do it.'

I try to explain the rules for naming a moon, but Willow isn't listening.

'Moonique. **Moontgomery.** Er... **JEFF. EASY!**'

It's getting dark outside.

I miss Hodgepodge.

'Artie?' says Willow, in a small voice. 'I'm really sorry I've been so angry and mean all day. You're right. I...I *was* a bit disappointed in Flummox. I just really wanted a cool monster to be friends with, and Flummox...' Willow pauses. 'She likes musicals better than actually good music, and...And she likes Arabella-Rose better than me.' Willow looks as if she might cry. 'But we brought Flummox here, and we have to take care of her. We can't let Wesley Crankshaw put her in a cage. We have to rescue her, even if she doesn't want to be my best friend.'

Suddenly, the bathroom door opens to reveal Wesley Crankshaw and Arabella-Rose. **Arabella-Rose is holding THE BIGGE BOKE OF FETCHING MONSTERS under her arm!**

'My darling Bella has obtained your book – or should I say, **MY** book,' says Wesley Crankshaw. 'She is so kind and tender-hearted that she's insisting I keep my end of the bargain and let you and

Hodgepodge go, before she will give it to me.'

He looks fondly at Arabella-Rose, who makes a soppy face at him.

Willow clenches her fists in rage.

Wesley Crankshaw scoops Hodgepodge out of the glass vase, and gives him to me.

The vase smells like vinegary socks. I hug Hodgepodge tightly.

Wesley Crankshaw stands back to let us out of the bathroom.

Arabella-Rose holds out the **BOKE** to Wesley Crankshaw.

'NO!' I yell. **'Don't give it to him, Arabella-Rose!'**

But she just smiles sweetly at me, and hands over the **BOKE**.

'Now then,' says Wesley Crankshaw, and starts to open the book.

Arabella-Rose clears her throat.

I hear a familiar squawk. And suddenly I can smell smoke.

Wesley Crankshaw shuts the book.

HODGEPODGE SHIFTS IN MY ARMS AND THE SMOKY SMELL GETS STRONGER.

Wesley Crankshaw narrows his eyes at me. 'If you think I'm going to fall for that trick a second time, then I've got news for—'

He is interrupted by the sound of sirens, faint but clear. The wail gets louder and louder until it's so loud it must be coming from just outside. The sirens wail again, louder this time, so loud they could be right outside.

Wesley Crankshaw freezes. **HIS EYES ARE WIDE.** Then he throws himself on the ground. '**FIRE!** Get down, everyone! Get down low and go, go, go!'

Wesley Crankshaw starts crawling on his hands and knees towards the front door.

I glance over at Arabella-Rose, who is staring at me.

She mouths the word **run**.

AND THEN SHE *WINKS.*

I don't have time to think about what's going on. I just hold tightly on to Hodgepodge with one hand, grab Willow with the other, and race to the front door.

There's nobody there. No car. No fire engine. No fire.

We run home as fast as we can.

Mum is waiting on the front doorstep. '*There* you kids are,' she says. 'It's dinner-time, come on.'

I quickly tuck Hodgepodge behind my back and we follow Mum inside.

David Cole has made roast lettuce with bacon custard. I slip food under the table to Hodgepodge, who munches happily. I'm not hungry. I'm too worried about Wesley

Crankshaw. Is he making a monster **RIGHT NOW?** Is he going to make a whole army of monsters, and take over the world? Is Flummox okay?

And why did Arabella-Rose tell us to run and wink at me?

Did she... *help* us?

'How did you kids get on with Arabella-Rose in the end?' David Cole asks.

Willow isn't listening. She looks small and sad.

'Um,' I say. I am not very good at lying. **'It's been a really long day.'**

Hodgepodge taps me on the knee. I peek under the table and he points into the kitchen. I look into the kitchen and see the edge of a fluffy antenna.

'Willow,' I say loudly, standing up. 'Why don't we clear the table?'

Mum beams. **'Such nice kids.'**

Willow sighs and stands up slowly.

I grab dirty dishes so fast I nearly break them. Then I hustle Willow out of the dining room and into the kitchen.

Flummox is there, perched on the sink, with a note in her beak!

Meet me in the Monster Club
~ A-R

CHAPTER 10

'IT'S A TRAP,' says Willow. 'She's working for Wesley Crankshaw! He wants to get Flummox and Hodgepodge.'

I think about the way Arabella-Rose winked at me. 'But then why would she send Flummox to us?'

'How else is she going to get us a message?'

I stare at her. **'The phone?'**

'She doesn't know our number,' Willow says.

'Oh...well, maybe—'

'IT'S A TRAP, ARTIE!'

Hodgepodge sits on the bench and opens a jam jar. He burps and farts at the same time. He looks pleased to see Flummox, who waves her antennae at him and clucks happily. I remember how scared Hodgepodge was of Wesley Crankshaw. He doesn't seem scared at all now.

'Do you two think we should go and meet Arabella-Rose?' I ask the monsters.

Hodgepodge nods, and Flummox flaps her wings. **Neither of them look scared, or anxious.**

Willow and I exchange **A LOOK**.

'Okay, then,' she says. 'Let's go.'

We go:

Through the East Wing.

Back to the piano room.

Through the secret door.

Along the passage.

Down the slide.

And find ourselves in the secret room again.

The stars on the ceiling are all shining, making the room look cosy and golden.

Arabella-Rose is waiting there for us, with her scrapbook on her lap, looking very pleased with herself.

Flummox flaps over to her and perches on her lap.

Willow takes a step forward, clenching her fists and opening her mouth to yell at Arabella-Rose, and for once, I'm *totally* with her. Arabella-Rose gave Wesley Crankshaw the **BOKE**!

But Willow stops.

Willow takes a deep breath.

Willow unclenches her fists.

'What do you want?' she asks, in a normal voice.

'To give you this back,' says Arabella-Rose, holding out her scrapbook.

Willow frowns. **'What?'**

'Well, I knew that Uncle Cranky was never going to let Hodgepodge go without the **BOKE**,' Arabella-Rose says. 'And… I thought about how I'd feel if Flummox lived with me, and someone took her away.' She stroked Flummox gently. 'The **BOKE** is about the same size as my scrapbook. So I ripped off the covers and swapped them over.'

Arabella-Rose opens up the scrapbook.

Inside are the familiar pages of **THE BIGGE BOKE** OF FETCHING MONSTERS.

I blink. 'You...ripped the cover off the **BOKE**?'

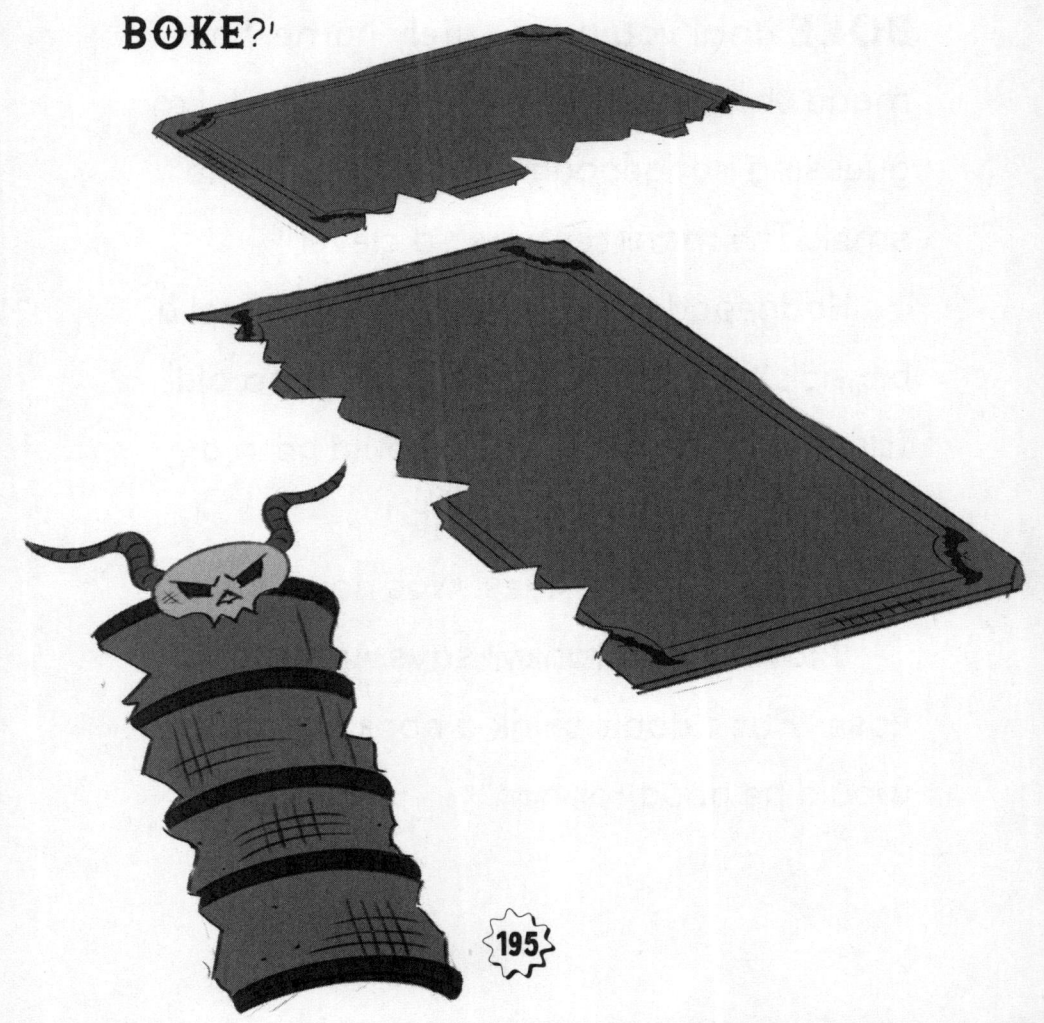

Arabella-Rose nods proudly. 'Then I asked Flummox to make a diversion, so Uncle Cranky wouldn't look inside the **BOKE** until you were safely home. She made the fire engine siren noises, but I'm guessing Hodgepodge made the smoke smell. The monsters are so clever!'

Hodgepodge farts happily, but I feel a bit sick. 'But...but...the **BOKE** is so old! It's a piece of history! It should be in a museum, and you *ripped* it?'

Willow rolls her eyes. 'Not now, Artie.'

'I love Uncle Cranky,' says Arabella-Rose. 'But I don't think a book like that would be good for him.'

'Was he very angry, when he realised?' Willow asked.

Arabella-Rose chuckles. 'Oh, sure. I told him how you two had been mean to me *all day*, and that stealing my precious scrapbook was just another horrible prank.' Arabella-Rose smirks, but I wonder if that sort of thing has happened to her before.

'So,' Arabella-Rose says, 'Uncle Cranky was mad, but not at *me*. Anyway, we had a good time looking through my scrapbook, then I sang him a song, and he was fine.'

I remember them sitting together while

Arabella-Rose was playing the piano and can't imagine she's lying about this part.

Willow clears her throat. 'Arabella-Rose,' she says. **'I'm really sorry I stole your fairy charm.** I can buy you a new one with the money I've been saving up for a new guitar amp.'

Arabella-Rose pauses, and for a moment I see how upset she is to lose her fairy charm. 'It's okay,' she says at last. 'I get it. You wanted to make a monster. I'm glad you made Flummox.'

Willow looks down at her shoes. 'I...' Her voice goes a bit wobbly. 'I think Flummox should live with you,' she says.

I stare at Willow.

Arabella-Rose stares at Willow.

Flummox and Hodgepodge stare at Willow.

'WHAT?' says Arabella-Rose.

'You didn't steal Flummox. She loves you. And… and you helped save us even though Wesley Crankshaw is your uncle, and I was pretty horrible to you.' Willow looks down.

Arabella-Rose looks happy and frightened and hopeful. 'Are you *sure*?'

Willow nods. **'I'm sure. Flummox belongs with you.'**

Arabella-Rose grins and steps forward, throwing her arms around Willow. 'Thank you, Willow.'

Willow makes a face at me over Arabella-Rose's shoulder and pats her back awkwardly.

Arabella-Rose lets go and Flummox flaps her wings and clucks happily. She hums a bright and happy tune at Arabella-Rose, who hums back at her.

'What about Wesley Crankshaw?' I ask. 'How can we keep Flummox safe?'

Willow shrugs. 'Wesley Crankshaw knows where we live now,' she says, 'so Flummox is no safer with us. But I trust Arabella-Rose to protect her.'

Arabella-Rose looks proud.

'And we can meet up in the Secret Monster Clubhouse,' says Willow. 'So Flummox and Hodgepodge can play together.'

'And I won't tell Uncle Cranky about your new monster,' Arabella-Rose says firmly.

'New monster?' I say.

'WHAT NEW MONSTER?' Willow asks.

'Well, I assume you made Flummox for you,' Arabella-Rose says to Willow. 'But she's living with me now. So you still need to make your monster?'

Willow grins, and I immediately feel nervous.

Arabella-Rose tips her head to one side. **'Do you hear that?'**

There is a funny noise coming from behind the green door. A kind of rumbling, gravelly noise, like a small avalanche.

Flummox lets out a terrified squawk, and Hodgepodge does an old-sock fart.

We all turn to face the green door.
IT SWINGS OPEN.

And a boy wearing a soccer uniform and a headband with a lightning bolt tumbles through. He looks up at the ceiling, which has the words **MONSTER CLUB** written in very large letters across it. He looks at Willow, Arabella-Rose and me. 'Where am I?' he asks.